Houghton Mifflin Company

Boston

For my godchild
Charlotte Kavanagh *H.A.*

For Jack Kearney *J.M.*

Library of Congress Cataloging in Publication Data
Allard, Harry.
Miss Nelson has a field day.
Summary: The notorious Miss Swamp reappears at the Horace B. Smedley School, this time to shape up the football team and make them win at least one game.
1. Children's stories, American. [1. Schools—Fiction. 2. Teachers—Fiction. 3. Football—Fiction] I. Marshall, James, 1942- . II. Title.
PZ7.A413Mg 1985 [E] 84-27791
ISBN 0-395-36690-9

Printed in the United States of America

Y 10 9 8 7 6 5 4

For some weeks now, gloom had blanketed
the Horace B. Smedley School.
No one laughed or threw spitballs.
No one even smiled.
Miss Nelson was worried.

Everyone was down in the dumps.

Even the cafeteria ladies had lost their sparkle.

Mr. Blandsworth was so depressed he hid under his desk.

"It's the worst team in the whole state," he said.

And it was true—the Smedley Tornadoes were just pitiful.

They hadn't won a game all year.

They hadn't scored even a single point.

And lately they seemed only interested in horsing around and in giving Coach the business.

"Why practice?" they said. "We'll only lose anyway."

"We're in for it now," said old Pop Hanson, the janitor.
"The big Thanksgiving game is coming up,
and the Werewolves from Central are real animals.
They'll make mincemeat out of our team."
"What's to be done?" said Miss Nelson.
"We need a real expert," said Pop.

That afternoon, while Miss Nelson was grading papers, she heard wild laughter.

It was coming from the teachers' lounge.

Coach Armstrong had cracked up.

"I'll make us a fresh pot of coffee," said Miss Nelson.

When Coach had calmed down,
Miss Nelson took him home in a taxi.
"You need a nice long rest," she said.

The next day it was announced over the PA
that Coach Armstrong would
be out for a long time with the measles.
"Who will take his place?" said the kids.

When Miss Nelson passed by Lulu's after school,
a serious discussion was going on.
"We need someone who can really get the team into shape
for the big Thanksgiving game," said one kid.
"Someone who knows how to get results."
"It's too bad Miss Viola Swamp isn't around," said another.
"Who?" said a kid who was new in town.
"You've never heard of Viola Swamp?" said the first kid.
"The meanest substitute in the whole wide world?
She's a real witch. She'd have no trouble getting results."
Mr. Blandsworth happened to overhear.
"Hmmm," he said.

LULU'S

"Hmmm," said Miss Nelson.
And she wasted no time getting home.

After rummaging around in her closet, she found
what she was looking for—an ugly black sweat suit.
Then she made an important phone call.
"I'll be right there,"
said the voice at the other end.

The next day Mr. Blandsworth announced
that there would be football practice as usual.
"Whoever it is," said the guys, "let's really give him the business."

The doors to Coach's office flew open and out stepped . . .

a lady in an ugly black dress . . .

"My name is Viola Swamp," said the lady.
"And I am here to get results."

“It’s Blandsworth!” cried the guys.
And they laughed him off the field.

“Oh, rats,” said Blandsworth. “How could they tell?”
Just then the guys heard the sound of squeaky tennis shoes.

"I am Coach Swamp!" said the lady in the black sweat suit.

"Holy smoke!" cried the team. "The Swamp!"

The team's fullback tried to pussyfoot away.
"Not so fast, Mr. Smarty!" said Coach Swamp.

"Wow!" said one of the guys. "Did you see that tackle?"

Coach Swamp was a real expert.
She put the team to work right away.

The guys had never done so many leg raises.
"More!" said Coach Swamp.

They had never run so fast.
"Faster!" yelled Coach Swamp.

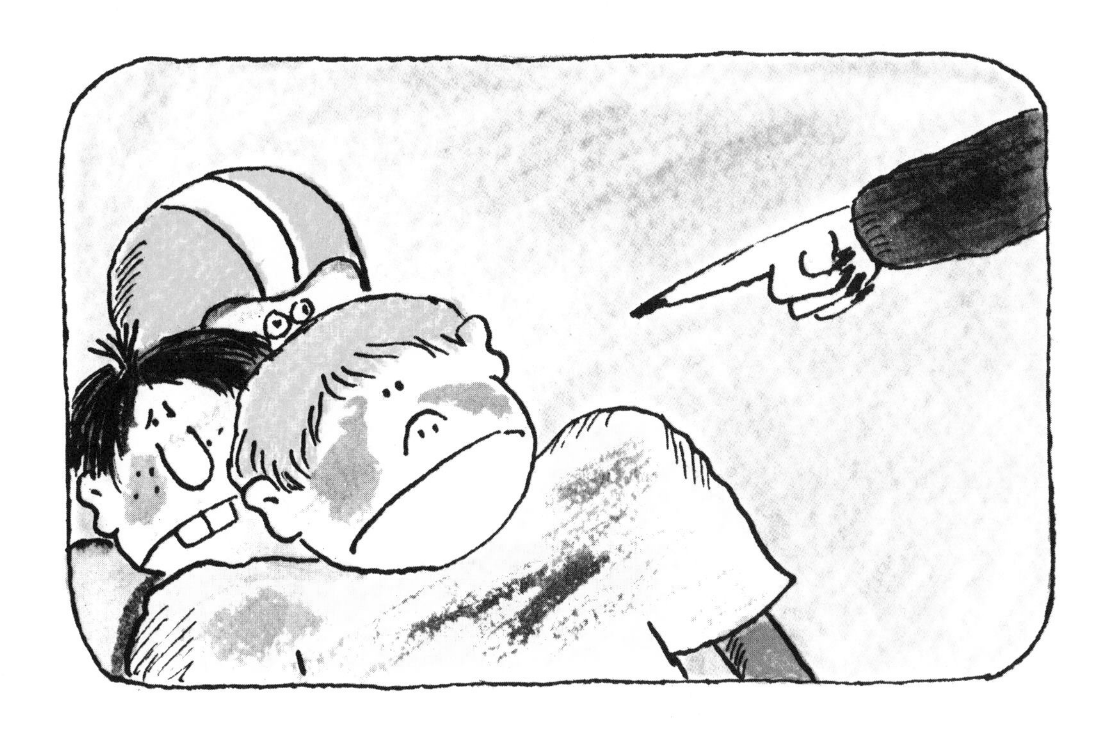

"This is murder," said the guys.
"Pipe down," said Coach Swamp.

In only a matter of days, the Smedley Tornadoes were looking better.

Coach Swamp really gave them the business.

Mr. Blandsworth was a little puzzled, however.

"Who *is* that Miss Swamp?" he said.
"Maybe Miss Nelson knows. I'll go ask."

Miss Nelson was busy grading papers when Blandsworth looked in.

"I don't want to disturb her," said Blandsworth. "She probably doesn't know, anyway."

Down on the field, Coach Swamp was having a little talk with the team.

"And don't ever think you can horse around again," she said. "Because The Swamp will be watching!"

When Coach Armstrong returned after his rest,
he was very surprised by what he found.
The guys played like a real team.
"How did this happen?" said Coach Armstrong.

"Er," said the guys.

GO TEAM
50

On Thanksgiving Day the Tornadoes clobbered the Werewolves seventy-seven to three.
It was a great day for the Horace B. Smedley School.

Mr. Blandsworth treated the whole team to hot dogs at Lulu's.
Miss Nelson went home tired and happy.

LULU'S

"Sometimes you just have to get tough,"
she told her sister Barbara.
"And by the way, thanks for filling in for me."
"Any time," said Barbara. "Any time."